Hi. My name is Adith,
but my Mum and Dad call me Prince Adith,
because they say I behave like a Prince.

I like going to Nursery and playing with my friends,
sometimes I get into trouble with my teacher
because I like to run inside the room and take
my shoes off.

Today is one of those days….here's my story.

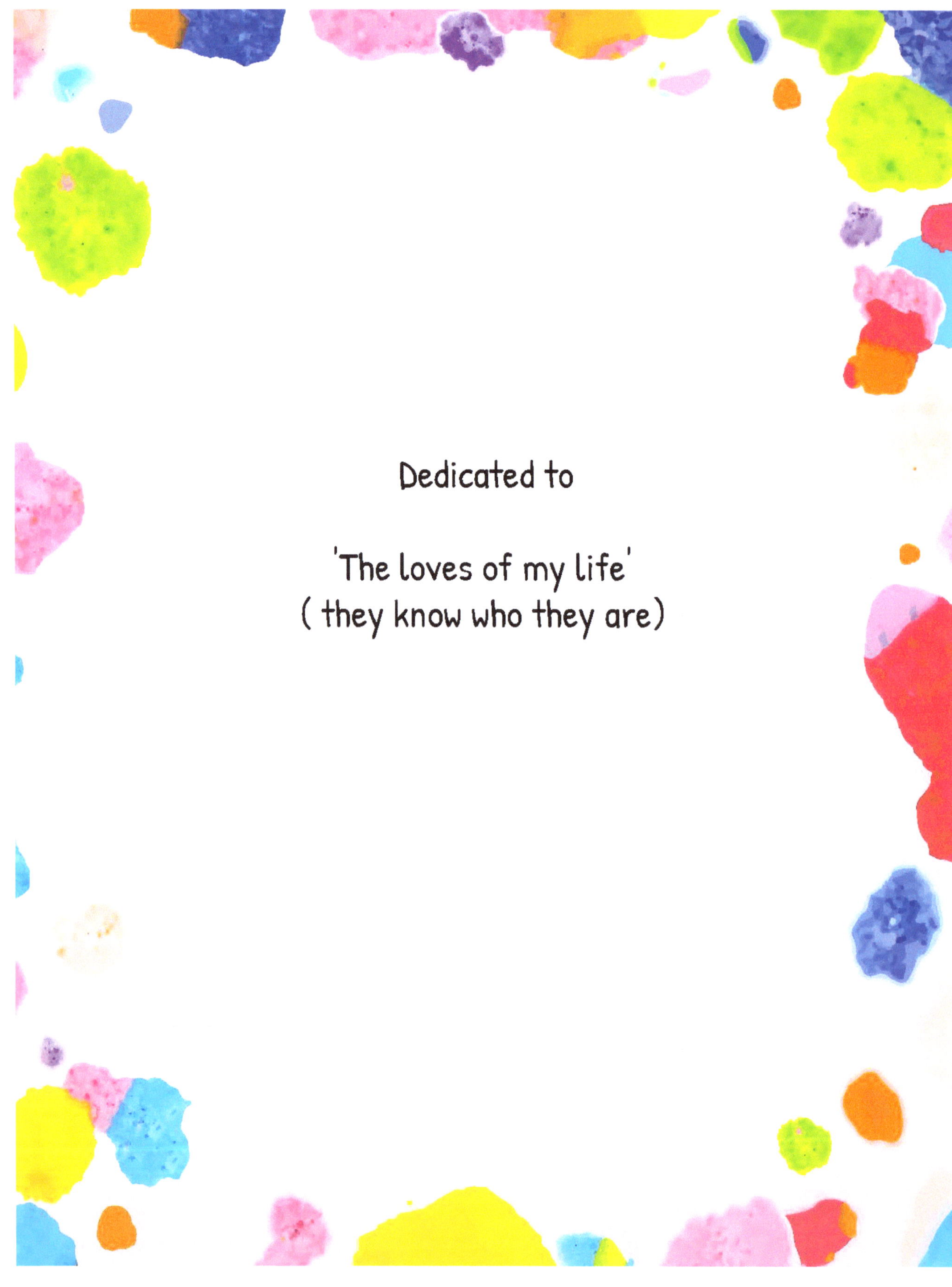

Dedicated to

'The loves of my life'
(they know who they are)

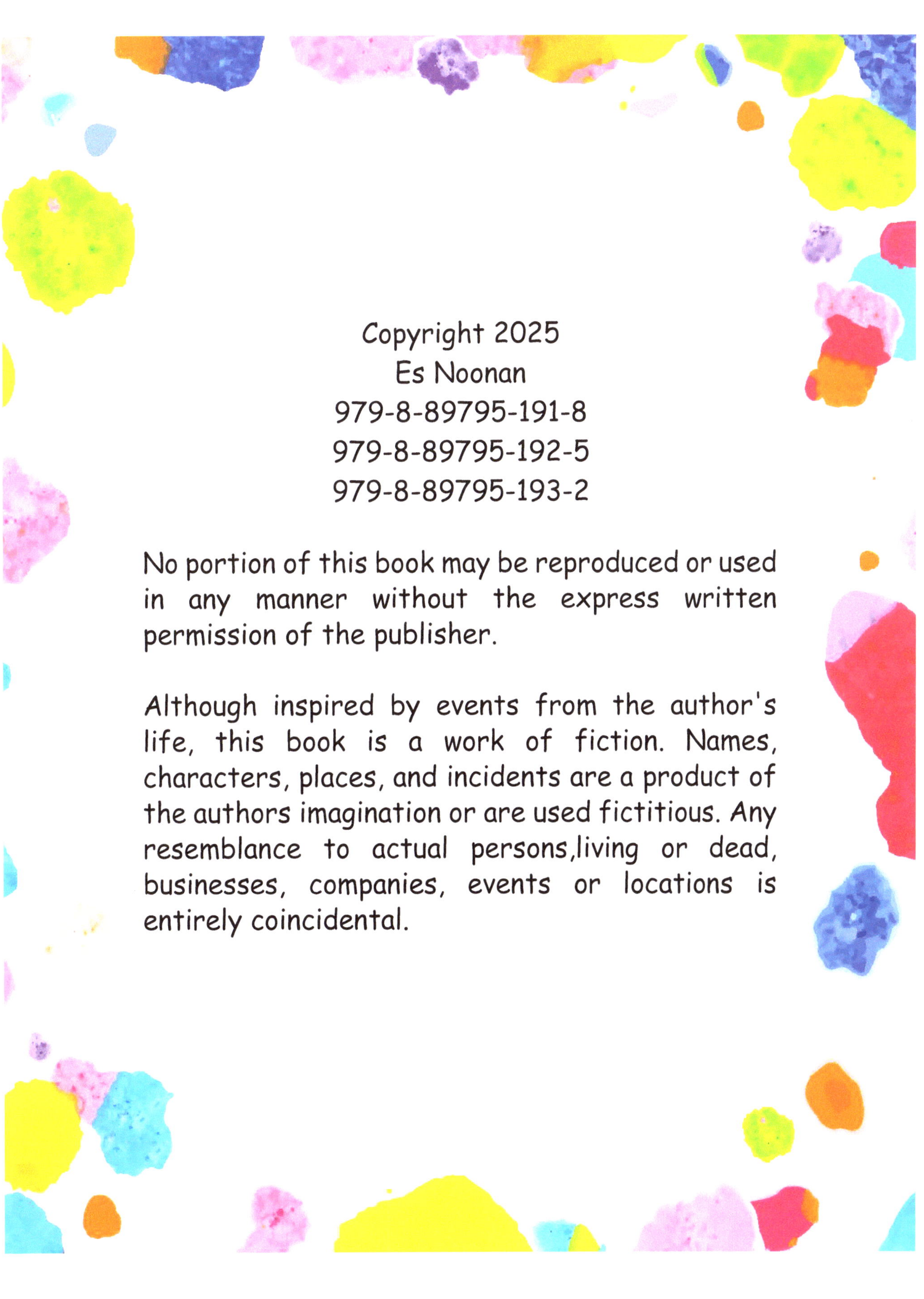

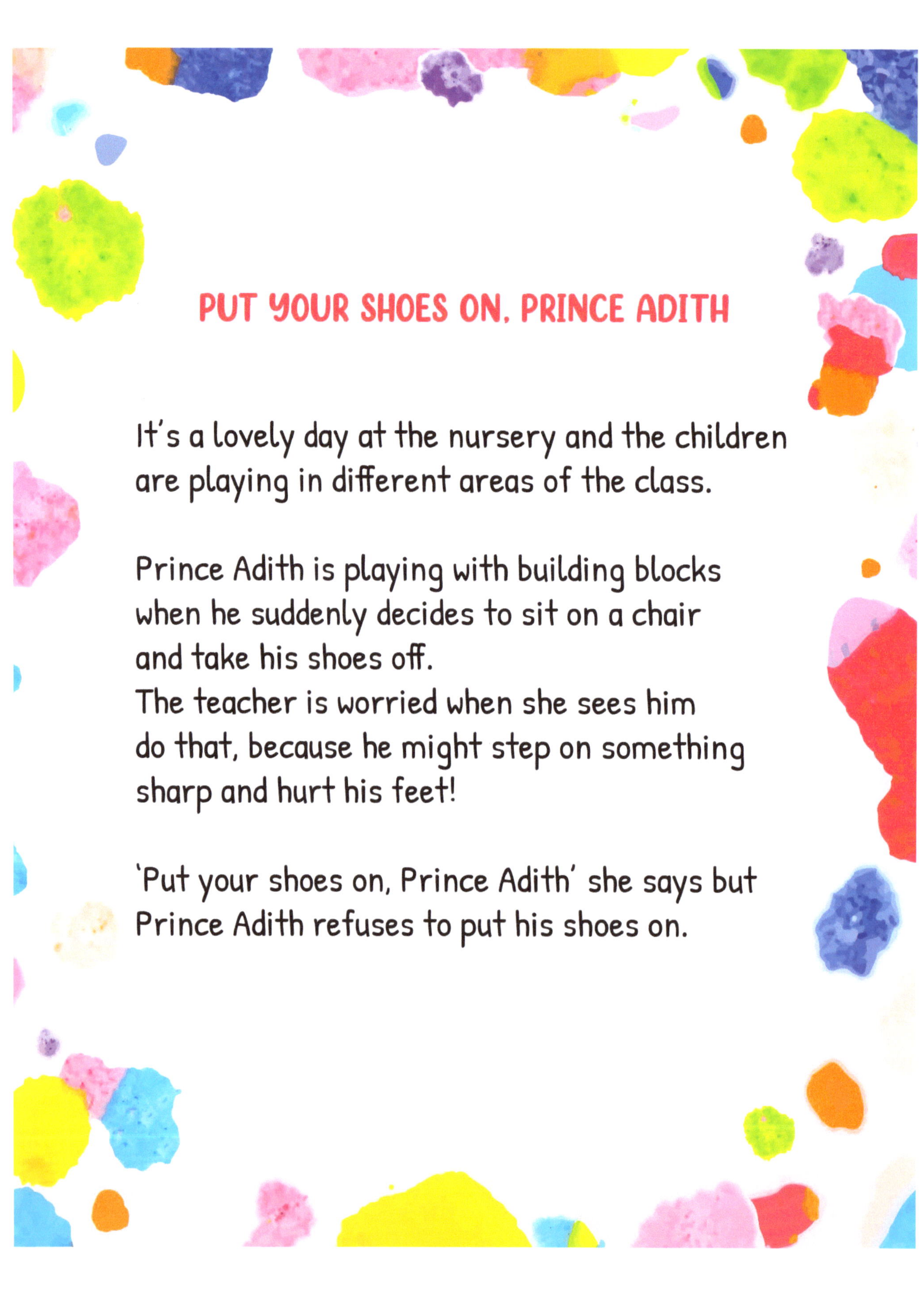

PUT YOUR SHOES ON, PRINCE ADITH

It's a lovely day at the nursery and the children
are playing in different areas of the class.

Prince Adith is playing with building blocks
when he suddenly decides to sit on a chair
and take his shoes off.
The teacher is worried when she sees him
do that, because he might step on something
sharp and hurt his feet!

'Put your shoes on, Prince Adith' she says but
Prince Adith refuses to put his shoes on.

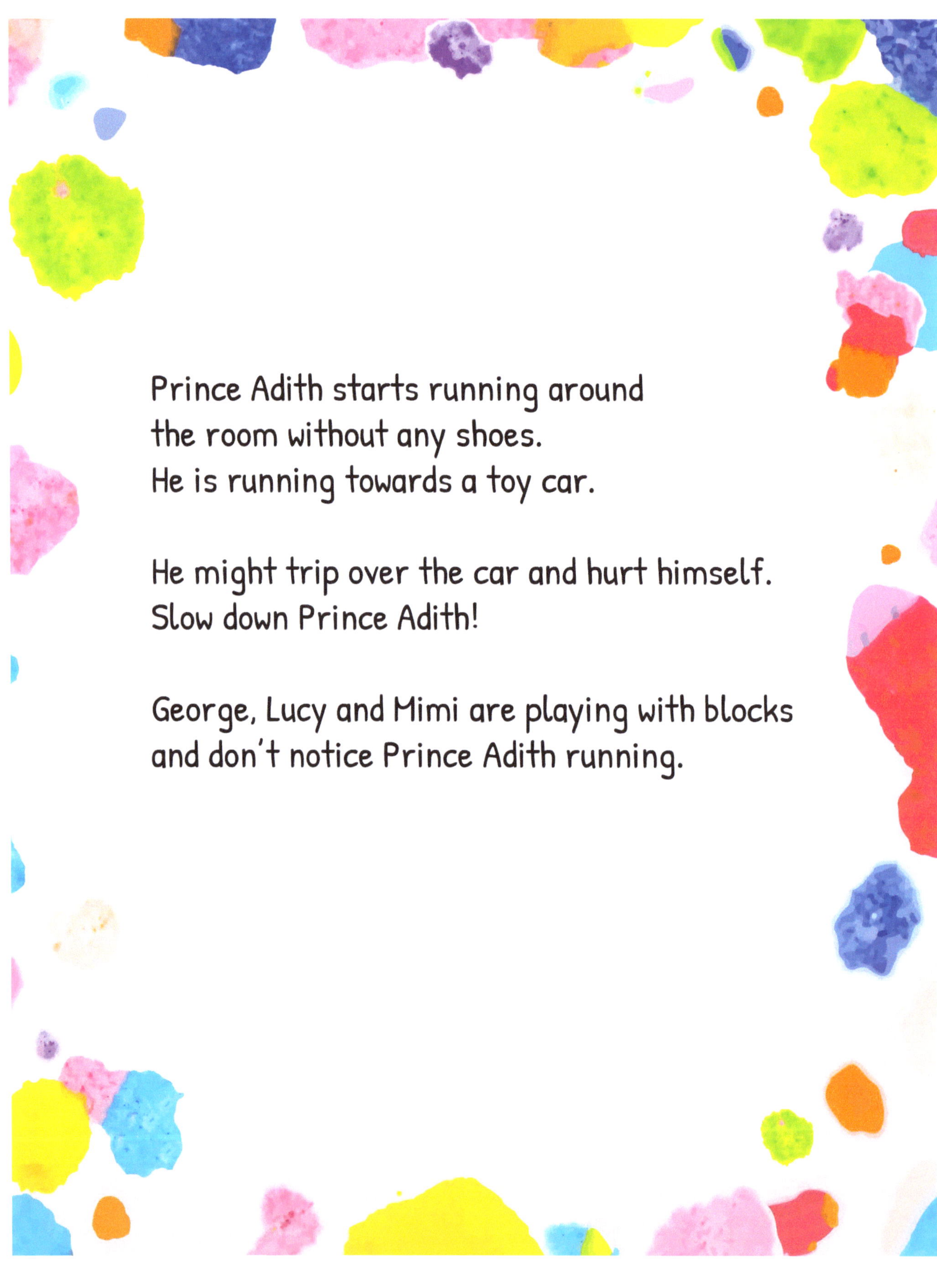

Prince Adith starts running around
the room without any shoes.
He is running towards a toy car.

He might trip over the car and hurt himself.
Slow down Prince Adith!

George, Lucy and Mimi are playing with blocks
and don't notice Prince Adith running.

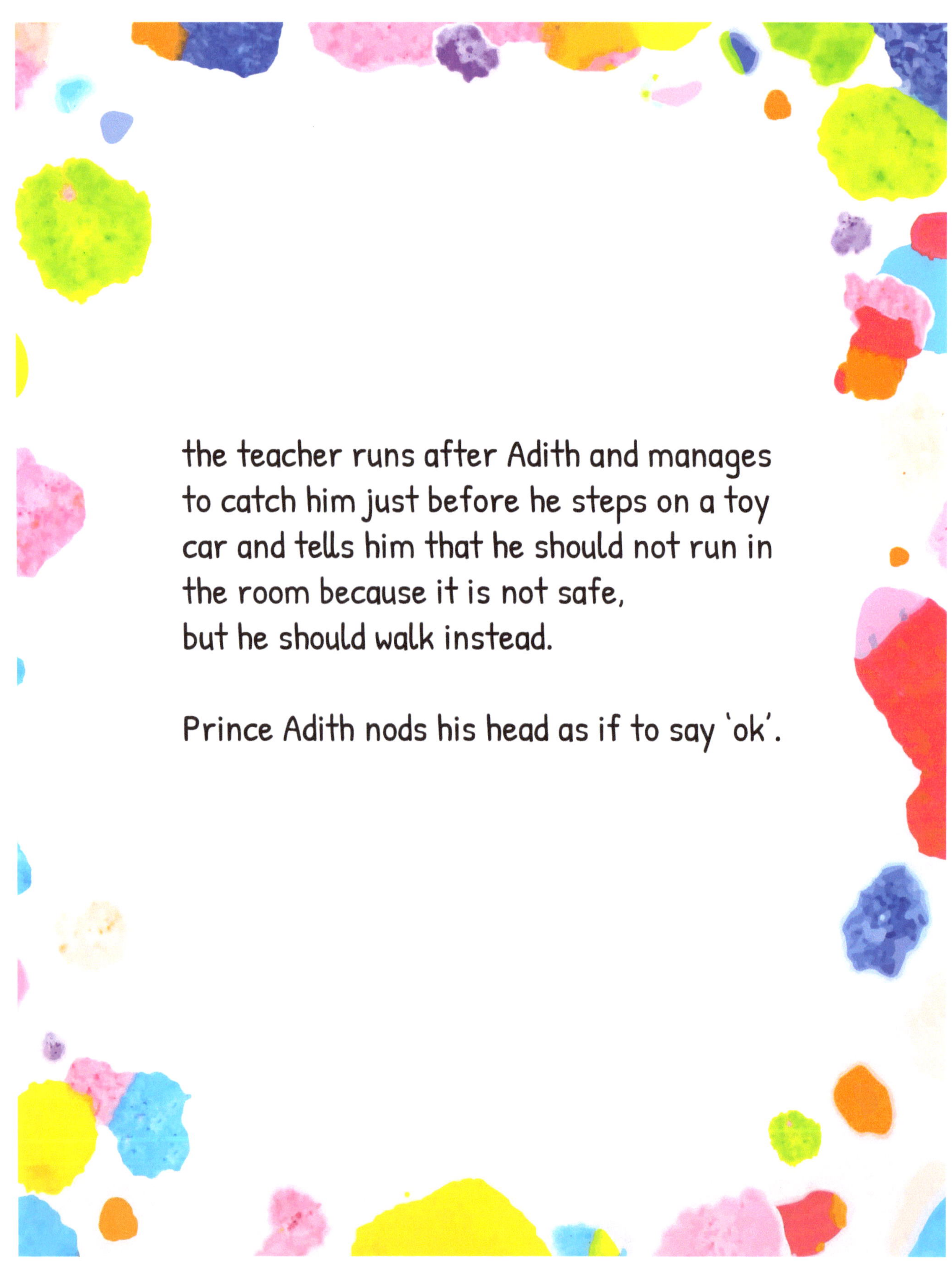

the teacher runs after Adith and manages
to catch him just before he steps on a toy
car and tells him that he should not run in
the room because it is not safe,
but he should walk instead.

Prince Adith nods his head as if to say 'ok'.

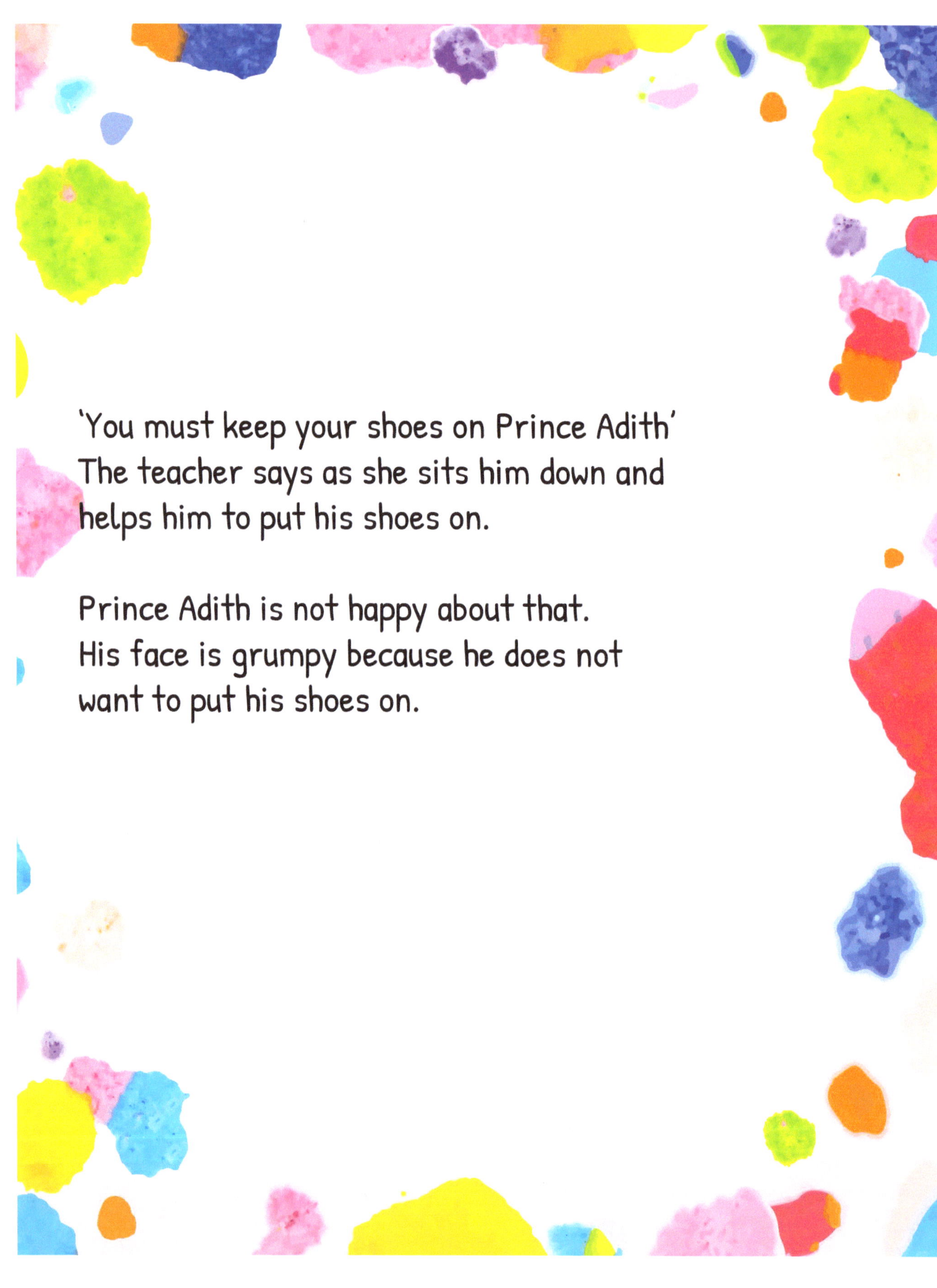

'You must keep your shoes on Prince Adith'
The teacher says as she sits him down and
helps him to put his shoes on.

Prince Adith is not happy about that.
His face is grumpy because he does not
want to put his shoes on.

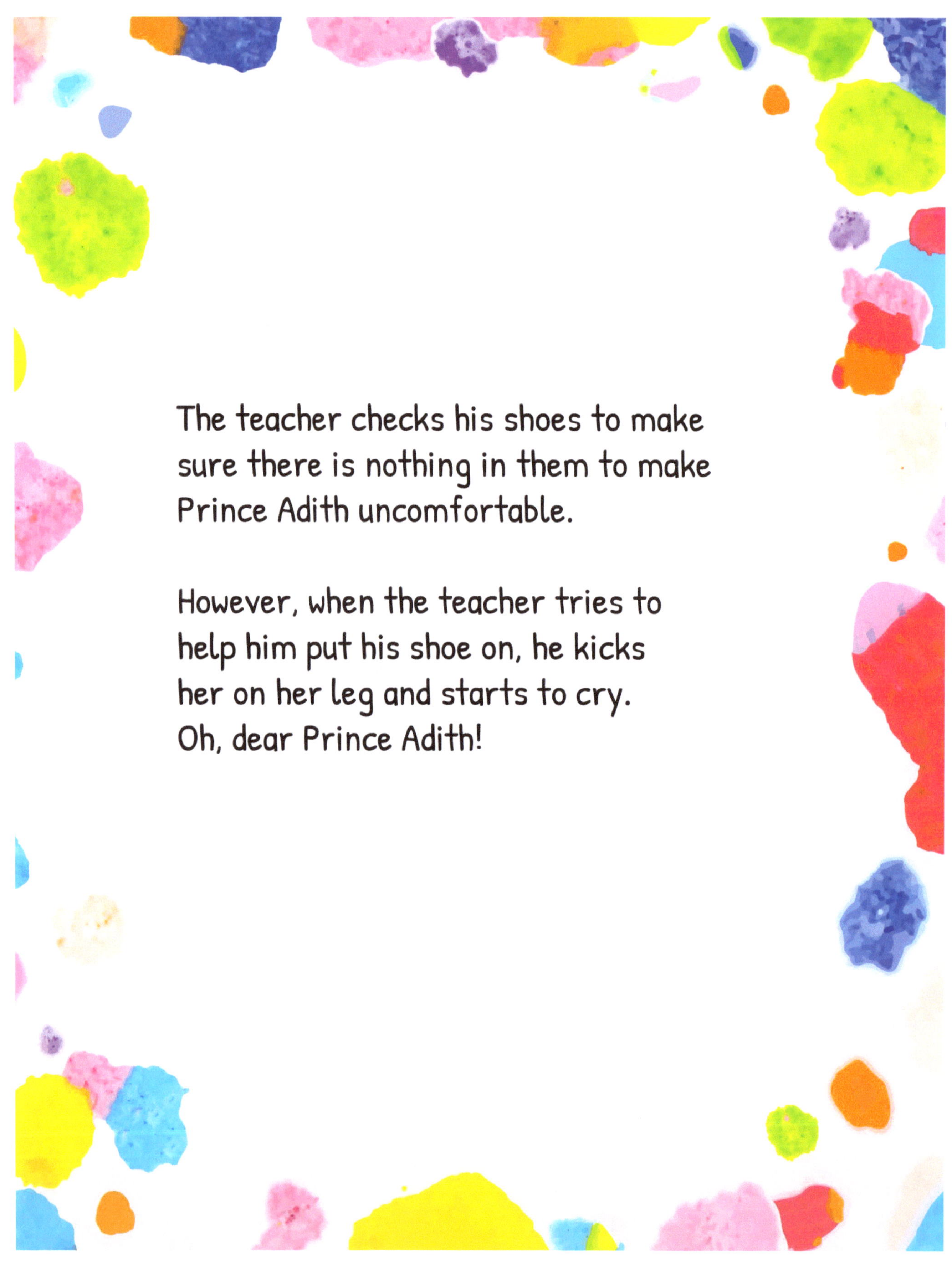

The teacher checks his shoes to make
sure there is nothing in them to make
Prince Adith uncomfortable.

However, when the teacher tries to
help him put his shoe on, he kicks
her on her leg and starts to cry.
Oh, dear Prince Adith!

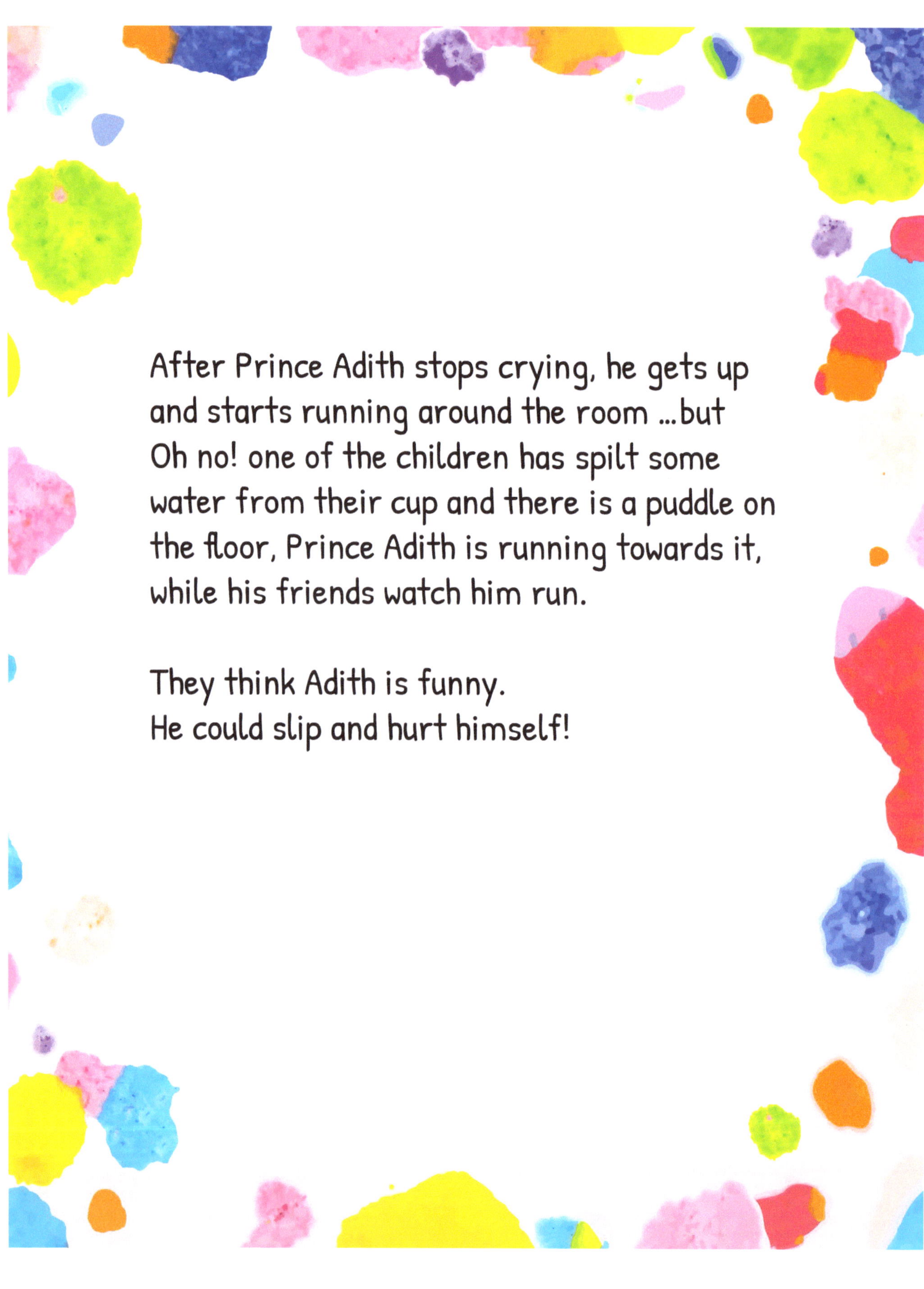

After Prince Adith stops crying, he gets up
and starts running around the room ...but
Oh no! one of the children has spilt some
water from their cup and there is a puddle on
the floor, Prince Adith is running towards it,
while his friends watch him run.

They think Adith is funny.
He could slip and hurt himself!

AR
OVAL
RECTANGLE
CLE
SQUARE
TRIANGLE

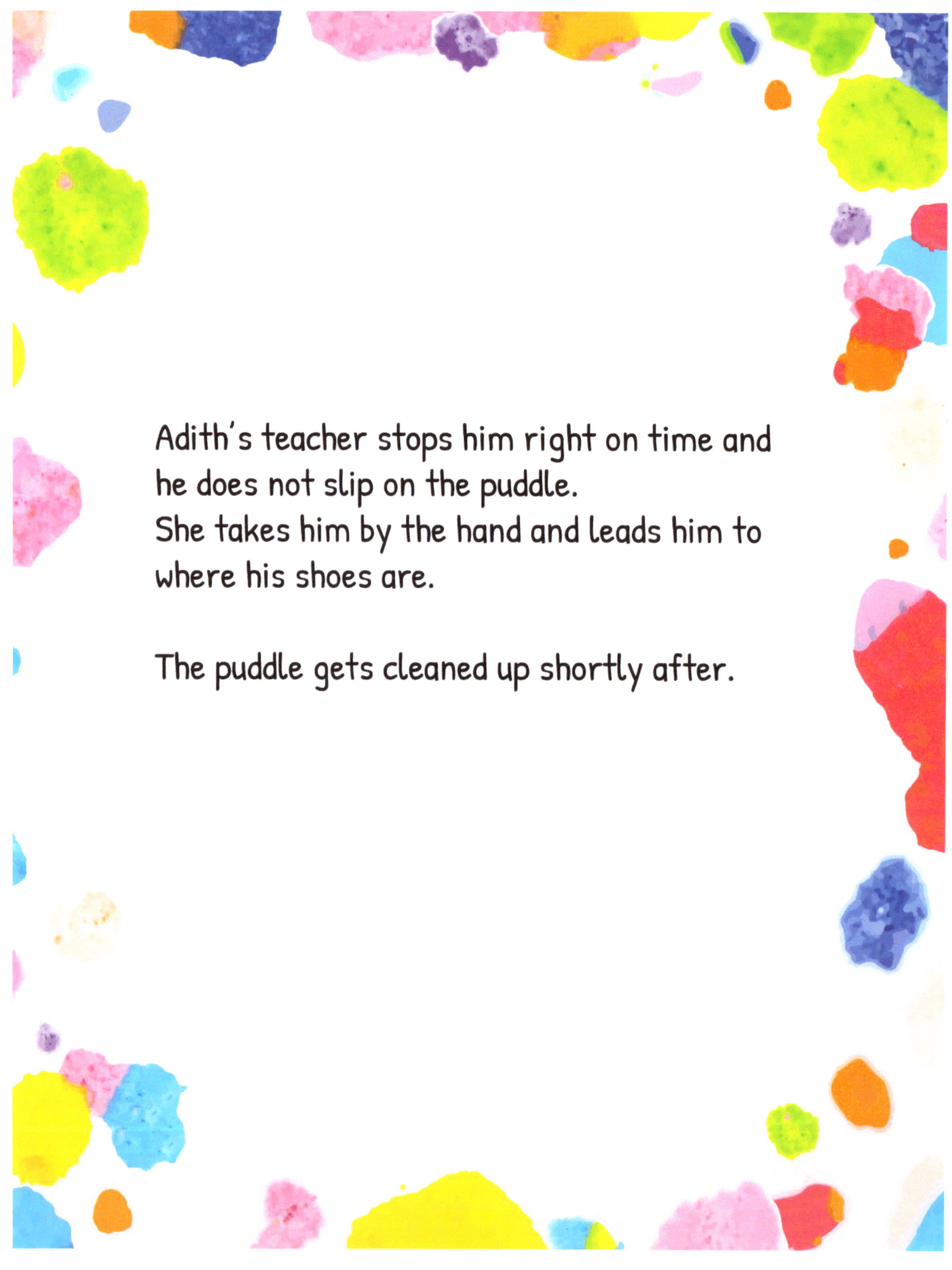

Adith's teacher stops him right on time and he does not slip on the puddle.
She takes him by the hand and leads him to where his shoes are.

The puddle gets cleaned up shortly after.

AR
OVAL
RECTANGLE
CLE
SQUARE
TRIANGLE
C

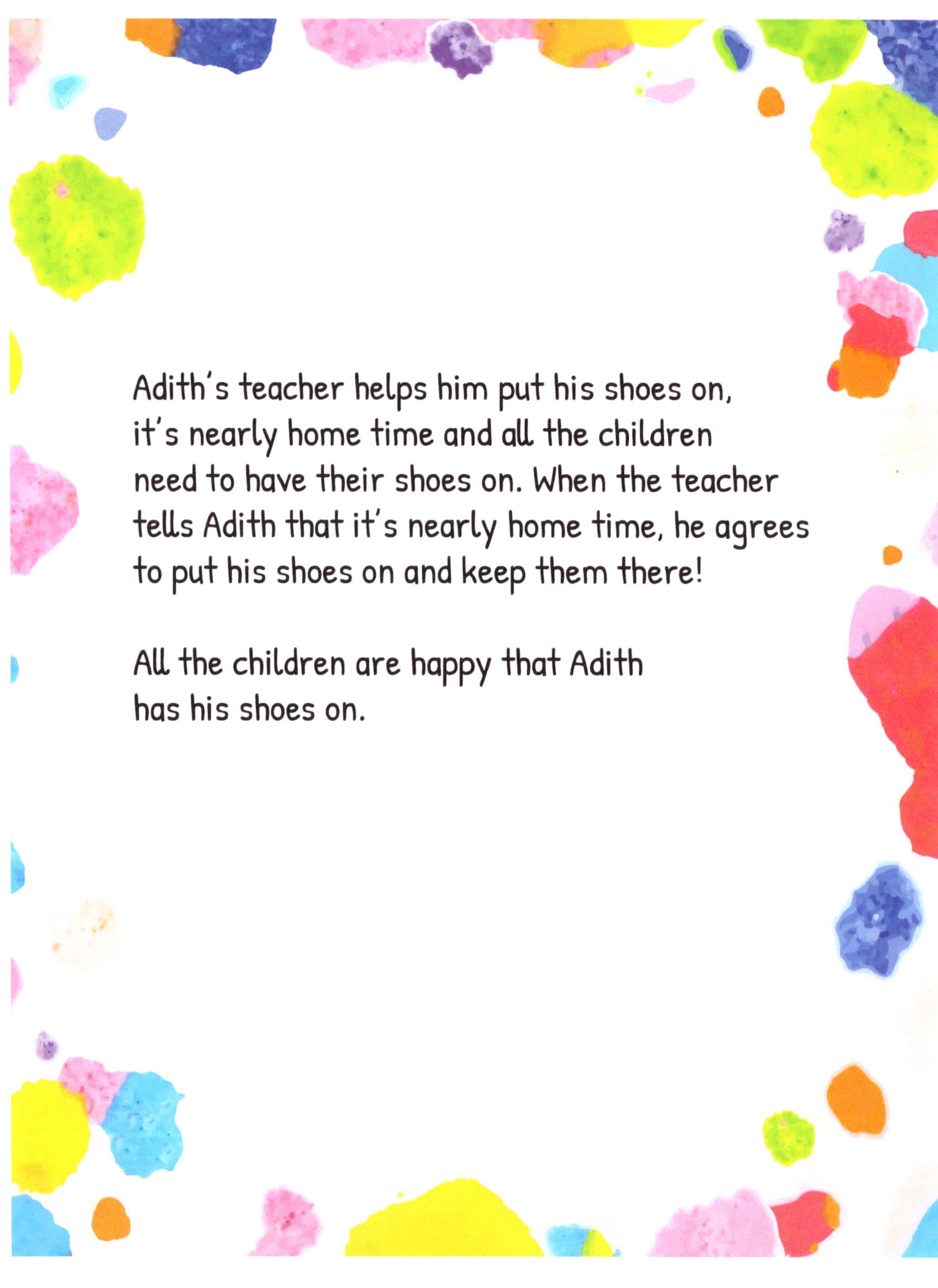

Adith's teacher helps him put his shoes on,
it's nearly home time and all the children
need to have their shoes on. When the teacher
tells Adith that it's nearly home time, he agrees
to put his shoes on and keep them there!

All the children are happy that Adith
has his shoes on.

STAR
OVAL
RECTANGLE
CIRCLE
SQUARE
TRIANGLE

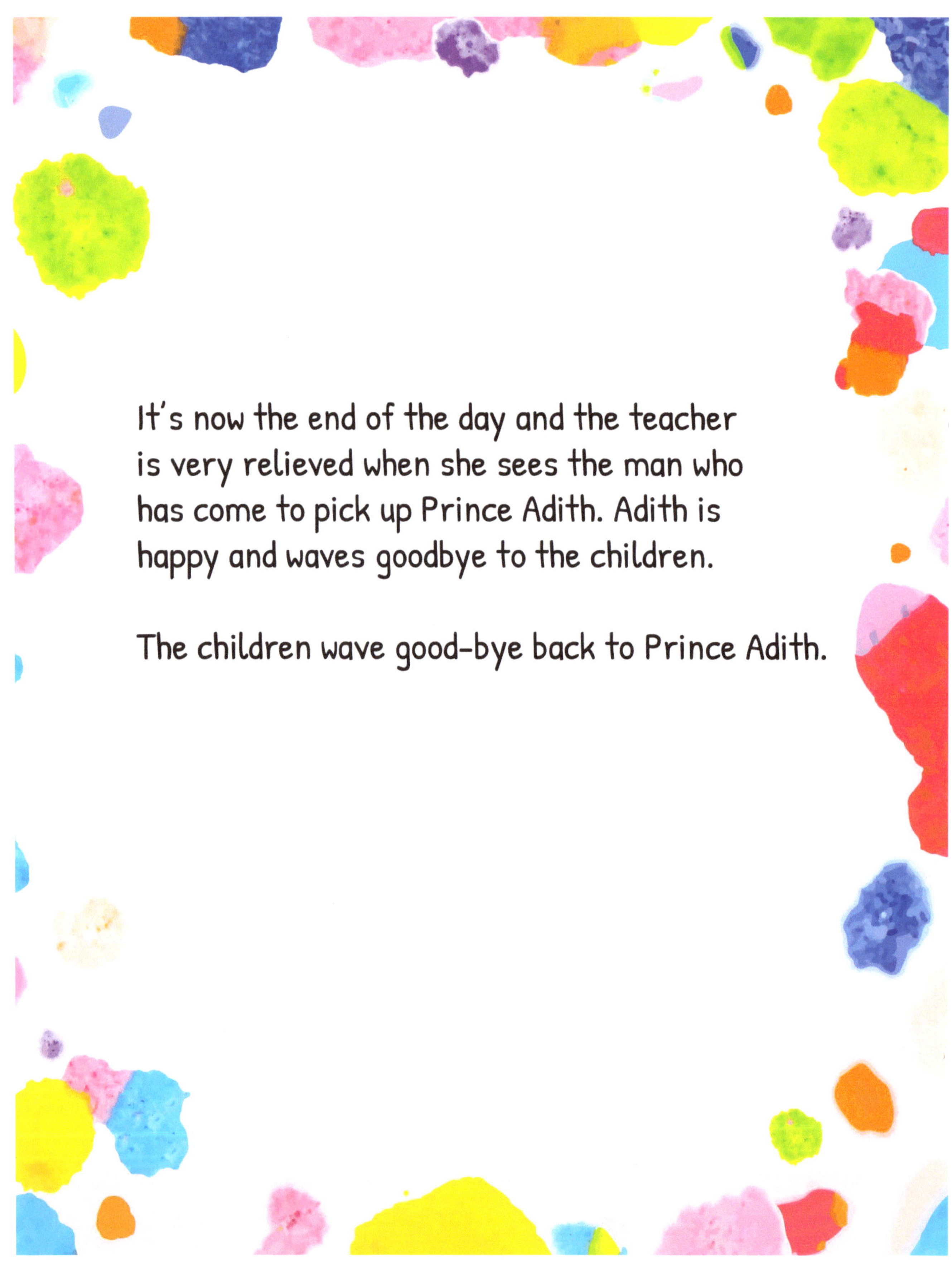

It's now the end of the day and the teacher is very relieved when she sees the man who has come to pick up Prince Adith. Adith is happy and waves goodbye to the children.

The children wave good-bye back to Prince Adith.

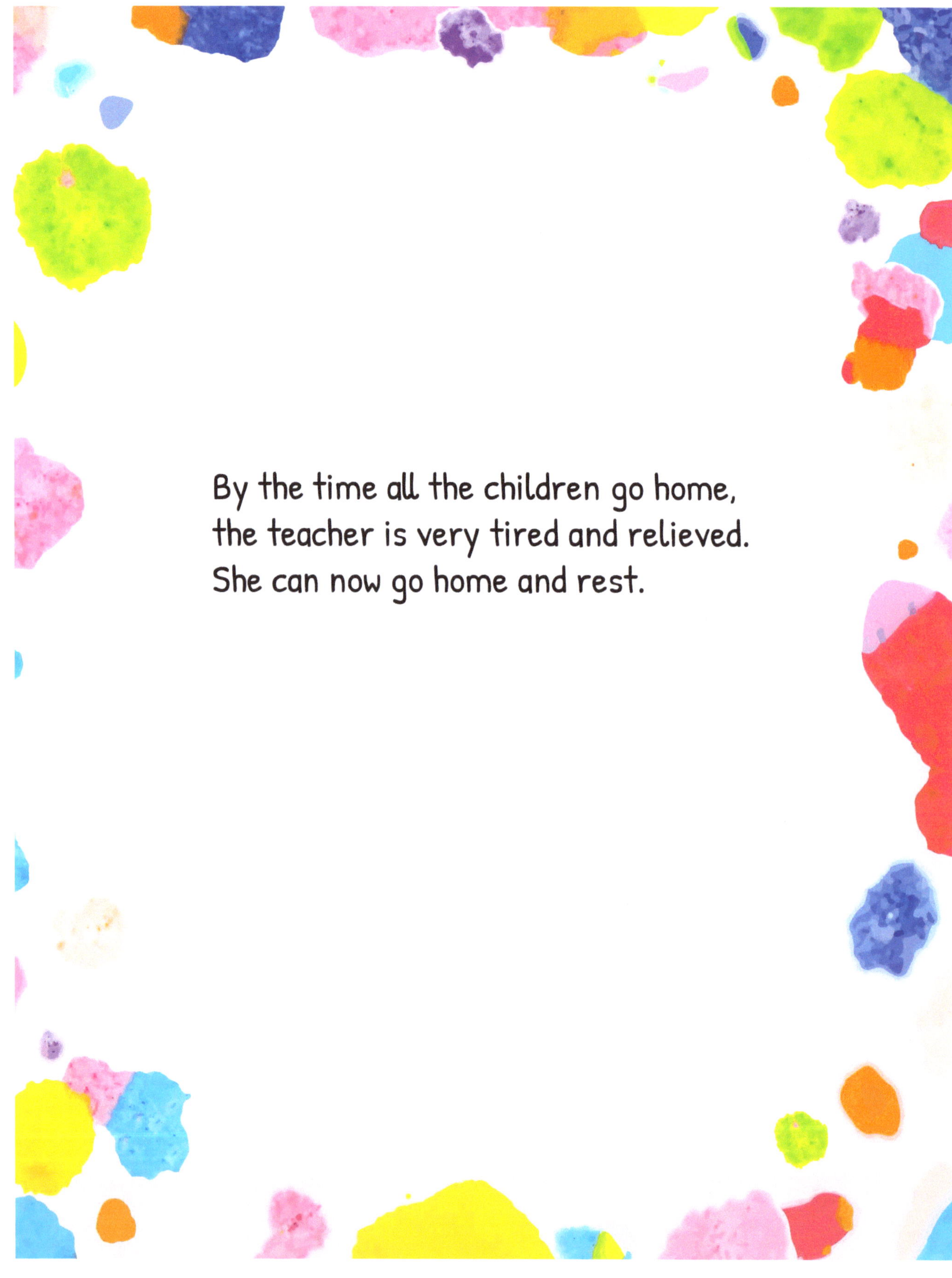

By the time all the children go home,
the teacher is very tired and relieved.
She can now go home and rest.

The End